For magic-makers Meg, Gene, and Gaddis   —C.G.

For Heidi, Godiva, Susing, and my nephew, Rey   —R.S.

Spanish-English Glossary

Clarita (clar-EE-tah): Little Clara

entrada (en-TRAH-dah): entrance

esposo y esposa (es-PO-soh ee es-PO-sah): husband and wife

gringos (GREEN-gohs): Yanks, Americans

El Mago (el MAH-goh): the Magician

al Norte (al-NOR-tay): to the North (the United States)

el Palacio del Educación (el pah-LAH-cee-oh dell ed-oo-cah-cee-OHN):
    the Palace of Education

El Papagayo (el pah-pah-GUY-oh): the Parrot

señor (sen-YOR): mister

la señora (la sen-YOR-ah): the mistress (or woman or lady)

Tía Mía (TEE-ah MEE-ah): my aunt

tortillas (tor-TEE-yahs): thin pancakes made of cornmeal or flour

Text copyright © 2007 by Campbell Geeslin ∗ Illustrations copyright © 2007 by Ryan Sanchez ∗ All rights reserved.
Published in the United States by Schwartz & Wade Books, an imprint of Random House Children's Books, a
division of Random House, Inc., New York. ∗ Schwartz & Wade Books and colophon are trademarks of Random
House, Inc. ∗ www.randomhouse.com/kids ∗ Educators and librarians, for a variety of teaching tools, visit us at
www.randomhouse.com/teachers

LIBRARY OF CONGRESS CATALOGING-IN-PUBLICATION DATA ∗ Geeslin, Campbell. Clara and Señor Frog /
Campbell Geeslin ; illustrated by Ryan Sanchez. — 1st ed. ∗ p. cm. ∗ Summary: Although her mother works with
a magician performing tricks, Clara finds real magic in creating art. ∗ ISBN: 978-0-375-83613-8 (hardcover) —
ISBN: 978-0-375-93613-5 (Gibraltar lib. bdg.) ∗ [1. Magic tricks—Fiction. 2. Painting—Fiction. 3. Artists—
Fiction. 4. Mexico—Fiction.] ∗ I. Sanchez, Ryan, ill. II. Title. ∗ PZ7.G25845Cl 2007 ∗ [E]—dc22 ∗ 2006016870
The text of this book is set in Columbus. ∗ The illustrations are rendered in oil paint. ∗ Book design by Rachael Cole

PRINTED IN CHINA

1 3 5 7 9 10 8 6 4 2

First Edition

Clara &
Señor Frog

by Campbell Geeslin

Illustrations by Ryan Sanchez

schwartz & wade books · new york

Watching from the shadows, I see Mamá being sawed in half. Her head sticks out of a box. The saw screeches as it cuts. A woman screams. Mamá smiles. I yawn.

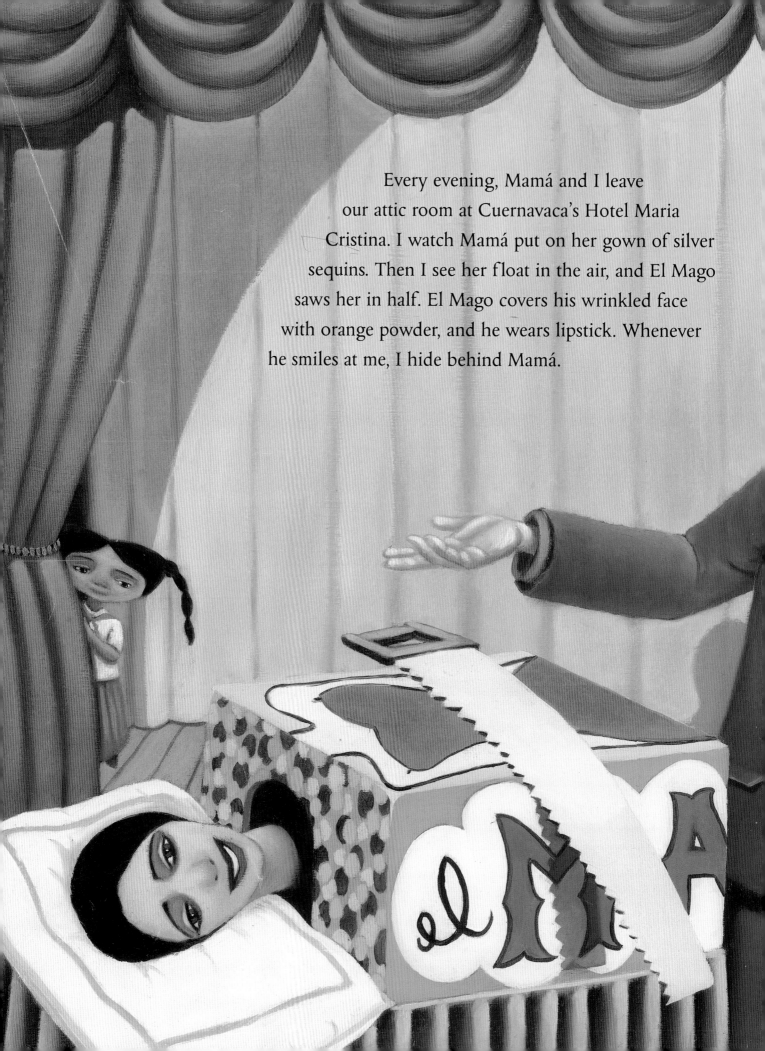

Every evening, Mamá and I leave
our attic room at Cuernavaca's Hotel Maria
Cristina. I watch Mamá put on her gown of silver
sequins. Then I see her float in the air, and El Mago
saws her in half. El Mago covers his wrinkled face
with orange powder, and he wears lipstick. Whenever
he smiles at me, I hide behind Mamá.

He always does the same things. Rabbits are pulled from a secret place in his tall hat. Doves wait in his pockets. A hundred silk scarves and paper flowers hide up his sleeves. Tricks, just tricks. I know them all.

One Sunday, Mamá's sister, Tía Mía, invites us to the house where she works. It is owned by rich gringos who have gone al Norte to visit relatives. We take a taxi.

When she sees us, Tía Mía stops sweeping the sidewalk, opens the door in the wall, and takes us into a pretty courtyard. The gringos' big pool is surrounded by pots of pink flowers and long chairs with pillows. Mamá says, "Now, this is the way to live!"

In the dining room we eat chicken baked in orange juice. There are hot tortillas and chilis and then pecan ice cream to cool my happy tongue. Yummm! Mamá says, "If you make me fat, sister, I'll lose my job!"

Tía Mía points to a framed picture on the wall. "The artist who painted that is famous," she explains. "La señora had him to dinner last month. He said my bread soup was the best he'd ever tasted."

"Look!" I say. "That fly on the painting thinks the watermelon is real!"

Tía Mía laughs. "No, Clara. That fly is painted on the melon."

I squint at the fly up close. "Oh! That's what I call magic!"

"Magic?" Mamá says. "A painted fly? Oh, Clara, every night you see magic at the theater."

"Mamá, you squeeze into one end of the box so you can't be sawed in half. You float in the air on a rod no one can see. El Mago just fools people. But the fly on that painting was so real to me that I saw it move. *That* is magic!"

After we have finished eating, I fall asleep on Tía Mía's bed. A bell rings and wakes me up. I hear a big voice boom out, "They aren't here?"

When I look out into the courtyard, I see Tía Mía at the front door. She says, "They have gone al Norte, señor."

"Who is that beautiful lady?" he asks, looking toward the pool at Mamá. His head is big. His eyes stick out. His belly is a barrel. This giant looks like a frog!

He walks over and sits down on a chair next to Mamá.
She looks like a little doll. When he whispers something,
she giggles.

The next night, after the last curtain, the man is standing at the stage door. His suit is green and rumpled. He holds out a bouquet of pink roses to Mamá and bows.

He grins, hands me violets, and tells me, "You must call me Miguel." But I think, No, no. You are Señor Frog.

We go to eat at El Papagayo, a restaurant nearby. As we walk to our table, all the people stop talking and stare at Señor Frog because he is a famous artist. Then they begin to whisper.

The next day Mamá and I take a taxi to a building called el Palacio del Educación. In a big courtyard, high up on a platform, stands Señor Frog. He is painting a picture that will cover the whole wall. The wet paint smells good, like fresh bread.

"Oh, it's wonderful!" Mamá says. "It tells the story of México!"

Señor Frog sees Mamá and climbs down the ladder. "You brought Clara," he says, and smiles at me. "She must be wearing white. I need her in white."

Oh? But I have on my prettiest dress!

"A white dress?" Mamá says.

Señor Frog pulls money from his pocket. "There is a market across the plaza," he tells Mamá. "Go buy the kind of dress a little girl from the country wears. Hurry. The plaster is drying."

Mamá hides me while I change into the new dress. When she steps aside, Señor Frog nods. His big eyes stare at me the way a frog looks at a bug before eating it. I shiver. Then he climbs back onto the platform. A boy hands him cans of colors. Everyone is so quiet that I can hear his brushes whispering as he paints.

Like magic, a little girl in white appears on the wall. She is holding a big bouquet of lilies. "That girl looks exactly like you, Clara!" Mamá cries.

But where did her flowers come from? Did Señor Frog just dream them?

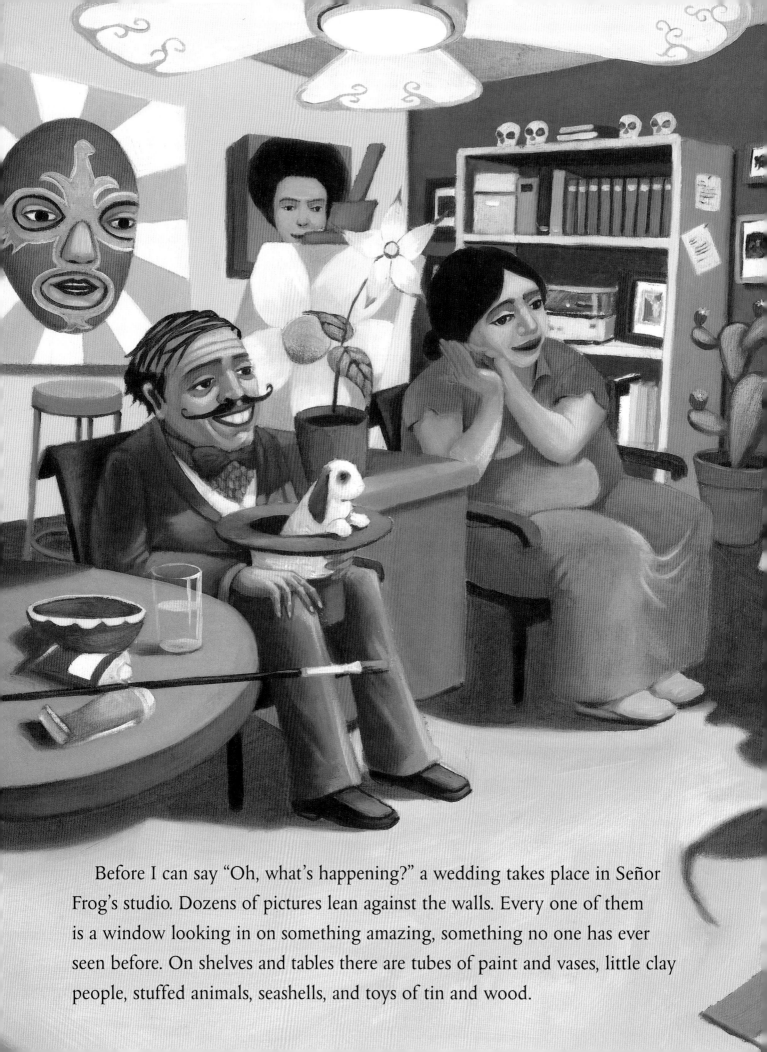

Before I can say "Oh, what's happening?" a wedding takes place in Señor Frog's studio. Dozens of pictures lean against the walls. Every one of them is a window looking in on something amazing, something no one has ever seen before. On shelves and tables there are tubes of paint and vases, little clay people, stuffed animals, seashells, and toys of tin and wood.

Mamá wears her silver dress from the theater. I wear the white dress Señor Frog bought me. The Mayor announces that they are esposo y esposa, and Tía Mía has tears in her eyes.

When Señor Frog asks Mamá to pose, she dresses up in a costume embroidered with great scarlet flowers. She says she enjoys standing for hours while he paints her. "It's the way he looks at me," she explains. "In his eyes I know that I truly am beautiful."

One day, Señor Frog asks me to pose. As I sit in his studio, time slows. The canvas trembles when he strokes on the paint. He moans softly as if his head hurts. Finally, he says, "Okay, Clara, come look."

The picture puzzles me. There I sit, but I am little and the chair is very big. I am holding a clay statue of a fat man. Green feathers hang from his face. There is a bird on my arm. "Why am I so little?" I ask. "Why am I holding that clay man? There is no bluebird in the studio."

Señor Frog wipes his brush on a rag and says, "I am not a photographer. I picture you in a dream, and then I paint what I see." He hands me a new canvas and a brush, then squeezes some brown paint onto an old saucer. "Now, show me something you see."

I look around and see a big shell from the ocean. It opens up like a flower.

Drawing with a brush is exciting. I hold my breath. I am careful. I make the shape of the shell on the canvas. The color flows, spreading out like something alive.

Señor Frog says, "See the lighter shade at the top of your shell? Rub the paint with this rag so the color becomes pale. Yes, that's it." He squeezes some red onto my saucer. Then he adds white. "Now mix those with your brush."

"It's pink!" I say. Everything that is happening seems magical. The pink makes me think of strawberry ice cream, and the shell is a cone!

"Make the color that is inside the shell," he says.

I add red so the pink is darker at the center.

Señor Frog sighs happily. "I thought so. When I married your mamá I got two models for my paintings—and one little artist, too."

Every morning now, I rush
to the studio where Señor Frog is working.
Some days he paints Mamá with blue flowers where her eyes should
be or shows her on a cloud in the heavens. She has the sun in one hand and
the moon in the other.
One time he shows me how a brush can make a line no bigger
than a hair. "I use this to paint the fuzz on a bee," he says.

I paint pictures too—
a portrait of my doll Amalia
playing with a lizard, a purple dog
sitting in a chair and drinking a bottle of orange soda.
Seeing the colors flow onto the canvas is better than listening to music.

Señor Frog brings more and more things into the studio. One is a green and yellow parrot. As I paint its portrait I teach it to say, "A thing of beauty is a joy forever." When an orange cat visits the studio, I paint its portrait and then add wings of silver lace like those on a dragonfly. One morning I paint an old boot of Señor Frog's with a yellow lily growing inside.

My pictures make Señor Frog laugh and clap his hands. "You and I know real magic, don't we, Clarita?" he exclaims. "We can make magic happen any time we want."